Doggone Christmas

A Polly Parrett Pet-Sitter Cozy Murder Mystery

Book 1

LIZ DODWELL

D1365396

Liz Dodwell

Doggone Christmas: A Polly Parrett Pet-Sitter Cozy Murder Mystery (Book 1)
Copyright © 2014 by Liz Dodwell
www.lizdodwell.com

Print ISBN-10: 1939860164
Print ISBN-13: 978-1-939860-16-3

Published by Mix Books, LLC

For Tracy,
Who makes every day a holiday

Liz Dodwell

Table of Contents

Liz Dodwell

One

ALL i WANT FOR CRISTMAS is TO BE A BUTFUL PRINCESS.

"Well, that didn't work out," I thought ruefully as I looked at the childish note. "How old was I when I wrote that? Six, maybe?"

I glanced at myself in the dusty old mirror propped against a pile of boxes. I'd never been a pretty child but braces had taken care of the crooked teeth and color-in-a-bottle gave highlights to my otherwise mouse brown hair, but there was nothing I could do about my one green eye and one brown. Oh, I'd tried colored contacts but they were so uncomfortable and it seemed rather like stuffing your bra with socks: they had to come out eventually, so what was the point? Now, at 27, I was resigned to the fact that I was passably attractive, sometimes sexy but never beautiful.

I was in the attic of my mother's home, the family home in Maine where my two brothers and I grew up outside a small town with the improbable name of Mallowapple. Two years ago my parents had split up, leaving Mom angry and embittered. Seb and Keene, my brothers, and I had been trying since then to persuade Mom to get out of the rambling old farmhouse that she couldn't possibly maintain, and she'd finally agreed. That's why I was in the attic, freezing my you know what off on a really cold November day – just after Thanksgiving - and making a start on clearing out thirty years of keepsakes while waiting for the realtor to arrive.

There was a sudden burst of high-pitched yaps mingled with a throatier bark. At the same time my mother's voice came from below, "Polly, he's here!"

"Coming!" I climbed down the attic steps then raced down to the first floor reaching the front door just as the man hit the bell, which caused the dogs to increase their volume and excitement.

"Enough!" I clapped my hands and gave 'the look' as three heads turned to me. Angel, a pitbull / Rhodesian ridgeback mix, Vinny, a miniature poodle and Coco, a toy poodle.

"Back!" I pointed to an old blanket on the floor and the trio obediently moved to it.

"Stay!" Then I opened the door.

The man standing there was nothing less than gorgeous. Close-cropped wavy brown hair, ice-cool gray eyes etched with laugh lines, and the most sensuous lips; he had a rugged air about him yet was dressed in a dark bespoke suit that had been tailored to complement his athletic frame, and a crisp white shirt, open at the neck.

Way to make an impression, Polly, I thought, feeling conscious of my dusty attic attire, no make-up and hair pulled into a severe pony tail. Still, I did my best to put on a brave face and smiled brightly at Mr 'Hottie.'

Unfortunately my dogs, though very obliging with the commands, 'Enough' and 'Back,' had never quite got the grasp of 'Stay,' and as the realtor reached out his hand to introduce himself, my mutts hurled themselves joyously at the stranger, knocking him to his back while they drooled and slobbered a welcome. The attache case he'd been carrying flew from his grasp, the top popped open as it landed and the contents were strewn across the front porch.

"Leave it," I shrieked. "Off, off!"

The dogs totally ignored me and continued their ministrations on Mr. Hottie, who actually wasn't looking quite so hot right now as he struggled to regain his footing. I grabbed Vinny and Coco, one under each arm and, herding Angel, managed to shove them back in the house and close the door.

Thoroughly embarrassed, I turned my attention to the scattered papers, snatching them up and stuffing them back into the attache case, which I then held out to the realtor who was brushing dog hair from his expensive suit. I wondered if I should mention the streak of slobber down his left pants' leg but decided it might be better to just apologize.

"I'm so terribly sorry. They're not usually quite that boisterous. They must really like you."

He glared fixedly at me and, to give him his due, didn't flinch at my odd-colored eyes as most people did. Of course, he might still be in shock so I pressed gamely on. "You must be from the real estate company."

"And you must be Mrs. Parrett," he practically snarled.

"No, that's my mother, Edwina. I'm Polly Parrett."

When he remained silent I babbled on, "Um, well, come on in. You won't have to worry about the dogs any more. Now that they've met you they'll settle right down."

Still he said nothing, just raised his eyes a little, so I opened the door and led him inside.

Angel, Vinny and Coco were relaxing on various items of furniture and, as promised, paid no more attention to us, though Mr. Hottie glanced a little furtively at them. At that moment my mother wheeled herself in. Much to my relief she was in her best greeting visitor mode. "Hello. I'm Edwina, how nice to meet you."

This time, Mr. Hottie did show momentary surprise. *He didn't know she was invalided and in a wheelchair.* Taking her hand gently he responded, "The pleasure's all mine. I'm Tyler Breslin, Breslin Realty Associates."

"Oh, we were expecting a Mr. Woodford, not the owner."

"He's one of my associates. I usually only handle the upscale clients (*What a snot! Upscale? What were we? Worthless?*) but he had a family emergency and I didn't want to leave you in the lurch."

"How very kind of you. We're honored."

Honored? My mother never spoke like this. She was acting as if Breslin was practically royalty.

"Why don't we get down to business?" I piped up before the syrup got any thicker.

"Yes. My daughter is an excellent business woman. She has her own company, you know. She operates a pet-sitting service."

Breslin turned to me. "And I can tell you're uniquely qualified for that." The acid was positively dripping.

I gave my sweetest smile, deciding not to rise to the bait, mostly because I couldn't think of anything suitably snappy to say. "So Tyler, how should we proceed?"

Was that a slight twitch at the corner of his mouth? My God, perhaps the man could smile after all.

"Why don't you give me a little background information, then I'll take a look around the house."

So I explained that we wanted to find something small and manageable for Mom and hoped to get enough out of the old house to give her a decent nest egg. "We figured we should get the house professionally painted and cleaned but didn't know if we ought to replace carpeting as well. Everything is terribly dated and my brothers and I plan to help with the costs but funds are limited."

"You're on the right track but let me quickly check something here." Tyler got up from the chair in which he'd been sitting and stepped to the corner of the room. Bending over, he pulled up a corner of the worn old rug. "As I suspected, there are genuine hardwood floors under here."

The floors weren't the only thing he exposed. His butt looked like a shag rug with all the dog hair he'd picked up from the chair, though it was still possible to tell it was a sexy tight ass.

"Is that good?" my mother asked. *Of course a tight ass is.... Oh! She was talking to Tyler.*

"It's great. For a relatively small amount of money you can get the floors refinished and you'll immediately increase your home's value and appeal. Hardwood floors are really in demand right now."

Mom looked pleased and I was glad to see her in a good mood for once. While she waited for us downstairs I took Tyler on a tour of the old homestead – six bedrooms, three bathrooms, a peek into the attic, then down to the huge kitchen, old-fashioned morning room and the basement.

"You can see why Mom can't go on living here alone."

"I assumed you lived here as well."

"No, I need to be closer to my clients, so I have a small place in town. When Dad was still here we'd talked about him and Mom one day retiring to Florida and I would take over the house to create a pet boarding center. There are more than 10 acres here as well, you know, and a huge horse barn with several other outbuildings. Of course, they're all in need of some work now but I just can't afford it."

Sighing, I ushered Tyler back into the living room where Mom had set up a pot of tea with a few cookies and the bottle of sweet cream sherry that she always kept for special occasions. *Oh, no!* That bottle hadn't been used since before Dad left, it must have turned to vinegar by now. And I was sure Mr. Hottie was more of a martini man.

"Do sit down, Tyler, and have a cup of tea," Mom gestured to the hairy chair. "Or perhaps you'd care to take a little sip of sherry?"

Tyler didn't miss a beat. "Sherry would be delightful, Mrs. Parrett." Graciously he accepted the glass; I took mine with extreme trepidation. Together we toasted to a successful sale, then we sipped. The stuff was absolutely ghastly. I gagged, Mom simply didn't know better and Mr. Hottie smiled warmly at Mom and said, "Delicious."

While we sipped we discussed terms. Tyler urged that we not over-improve the property because we risked not getting the money back in a sale. He told us he would work up some comps and get back to us with a suggested sale price in a couple of days, then he stood to leave. The dogs sensed something was up and came to say goodbye. Surprisingly, Tyler accommodated them by scratching their ears and three tails wagged happily.

"Thank you," I said as I walked him to the door, "for being so nice to my mother and drinking that awful sherry."

"Your mother is a lovely lady who's had a really rough time. I enjoyed meeting her." His smile this time crinkled those laugh lines round his eyes. *Mr Hottie just went way back up in my estimation.*

Liz Dodwell

Two

In the few minutes it had taken for me to see Tyler out, Mom had reverted to bitter mode.

"It's not fair that I'm being forced out of my home, especially with the holidays coming. If my disability money wasn't so paltry I could fix the place up. Your father should do something. It's his fault anyway that this is happening."

Oh, Lord.

My mother had given riding lessons and been a fairly successful competitor in show jumping until a fall left her paralyzed below the waist. It also left her angry and depressed. Unable to ever ride again she couldn't bear to keep her beloved horses or continue with her business. Dad was a trooper and took over the household chores along with the extra care Mom's condition required. Then the lousy economy caught up and he was laid off from the accounting company where he'd worked for years. He struggled to make ends meet by working as a private consultant but, with the loss of health care insurance Mom's incessant quibbling and ungrateful attitude became too much. He took off with the pharmacist who regularly filled Mom's prescriptions. Though I was hurt and angry at his abandonment at first, having taken over the role of caregiver I had come to sympathize. And to give Dad his due, the pharmacist wasn't some 20-something but a mature and intelligent woman.

"Mom, we've been through this before. Dad signed the house over to you and it has a lot of equity. With the proceeds from the sale you should be able to live comfortably for the rest of your life." *And maybe my life will be a little easier. I won't have to spend an hour a day driving out here.*

"But it's our family home. There are so many memories." *She had a point there.* Then she started to cry.

I hated to leave her like this but I had a dog-walk to get to. Fortunately, at that moment one of my cats appeared and jumped on her lap. Cappy (short for Cappuccino because he had a strip of white hair above his mouth that looked like a milk mustache) resided with my mother. Actually, I had six cats but my little house in town was already maxed-out with pets so Lief, Ollie and Cappy stayed with Mom. So far it had been a perfect arrangement. My mother loved the cats' company and they had the run of the whole house. I was concerned how things would work when Mom moved though, and realized I hadn't mentioned that to Tyler. I'd have to give him a call.

Taking advantage of Cappy's distraction I hastily departed. I'd be back in the morning anyway, to help Mom get dressed. Five days a week she had an aide who came in to bathe her and get her ready for the day. The rest of the time it was mostly up to me, and tomorrow the aide was off. Seb lived 1,000 miles away; Keene's home was a two-hour drive from here but he and his wife tried to visit every other weekend and would stay overnight.

On the way to my house to drop off the dogs before my scheduled walk I dialed Tyler's number. It went straight to voicemail and I was annoyed to find myself a little disappointed that Mr Hottie himself hadn't answered. I left a message that we'd need a place where three cats would be OK then set aside all thoughts of real estate and got back to business.

Liz Dodwell

Three

I'd enjoyed the dog walk. I don't do a lot of hands-on work these days but one of my team of six was on vacation this week so I was filling in.

Back in my home office (OK, it's the kitchen table) the time sheets were staring at me. I hated paperwork. One of these days I'd be able to afford an assistant to take care of such things; for now I just had to suck it up. I glanced at the clock. I should be able to finish by about seven, then I could reward myself with some of the pistachio gelato that was calling me from the freezer. Five minutes into my calculations the phone rang. I didn't recognize the number so I answered in my peppy work voice, "Pets and People, Too. This is Polly, can I help a pet or a person today?"

"Um, actually, I'm calling to help you." *Tyler!*

"Oh, hello. Is this the realtor?" *The realtor?* Why didn't I just say the man's name? Why was I a blithering idiot all of a sudden?

"Yes, it's Tyler." Emphasis on his name. "Is this a bad time?"

Get a grip, Polly. I took a calming breath. "Not at all. You saved me from a mountain of paperwork. At least, temporarily."

He laughed – I liked the sound.

"Polly, I got your message and I've found a couple of properties that might be of interest. Also, I've been running some figures that I'd like to go over with you. Do you think you might have a couple of hours tomorrow?"

"I have a really full calendar for the rest of the week. Let me look….."

"Great." He interrupted. "Then let's talk over dinner tonight. I'll pick you up at seven."

"Uh, um, well, I'm not sure…." Mr Hottie was asking me on a date?

"That's not a problem, is it? Strictly business, of course."

"Of course," I said coolly and gave him my address.

Annoyed at caving so easily to Tyler's imperious assumption that I'd be readily available when it suited him, I consoled myself with the fact that at least I'd get a decent dinner – and I'd make him pay! *Dinner! Oh, my god. Where would he take me?*

Tyler Breslin, CEO of Breslin Realty Associates did not strike me as a burger and beer type of guy and with my seriously limited finances that's about all I was familiar with. Hell, nearly all my clothes were 'pet' clothes – scruffy and comfortable gear that could handle dog drool or parrot poo. I didn't have a thing to wear amongst the country club set if we went somewhere swanky. For that matter, I was still in my dirty old dungarees and sweat shirt from Mom's attic and, beginning to panic, I realized I only had about an hour to get ready! And the house was a wreck!

I raced for the shower, shedding clothes on the way. Exactly fifty minutes later I was washed, coiffed and dressed in my only decent pair of black skinny jeans with a panther-print Lanvin top that I'd picked up for $100 in a consignment store a year before. For that price I figured it was a steal, though I really hesitated to shell out so much money. The fact that it was a charity store to benefit abused animals tipped the decision in favor of buying. If Tyler was really dressed up I figured I could tell him I assumed our 'business' dinner would be casual and suggest somewhere middle-of-the-road that would suit us both.

Just then the dogs' ears' pricked up. *Can't the man be fashionably late?*

I grabbed the papers off the table along with the clothes I'd strewn on the floor and hid them in the kitchen cupboards. Fortunately that was no problem as I only had a few cans of food and a couple of cracked coffee cups. As I stepped into my shoes there was a knock on the door.

"Just a minute," I yelled over the dog's barking.

I'd opted for three-inch heels. I'm only five two and Tyler must be at least six two so I felt I needed an advantage. Maybe it wasn't such a good idea, though. My life was spent running around in sneakers and the sudden thrust into the stratosphere had me a little wobbly. I tottered to the door.

Tyler stood there in old Levis, boots and a down jacket. As the dogs rushed out he was ready for them and got down on one knee to scruff their necks. From that vantage point his gaze moved from my feet, slowly up my body 'til he was looking directly into my eyes when he grinned mischievously.

"You might want to reconsider those shoes. There's a chance of snow tonight..... You look really great, by the way."

I didn't know whether to be annoyed or flattered so I just pirouetted on my stilettos intending to flounce away and let him see how good I looked in tight jeans. Only I'd forgotten everything I ever learned at my childhood ballet classes and my graceful pirouette became a klutzy lurch as my heel caught on the doormat and down I went. The dogs, of course, loved this new game and this time I was the one to be slobbered over.

"Are you OK?" I swear he was trying not to laugh.

Pink with embarrassment I shoved Angel away, "Of course I'm fine." *Like I do this all the time?*

Tyler leaned down, took hold of me under the arms and lifted me to my feet as if I weighed no more than a mouse. *Wow, he must really work out.* Then he picked something off the floor and held it out to me.

"My heel. It broke off. Now I'll have to wear flats."

"It's probably safer that way." And this time, there was no doubt he was laughing.

Four

Dinner was in a small Indian restaurant that had recently opened up in town. The aroma of warm spices was wonderful and the décor a sumptuous mix of dark woods, rich reds and golds. There were no chairs. Instead, the tables were low and flanked with even lower benches or surrounded with cushions. I was just thinking it was lucky I wasn't in three-inch heels when we were instructed to leave our shoes in a cubby near the entrance. *OK, then.*

Only a handful of tables were occupied and we were seated in a quiet corner where the lights were low. I figured that was good because I looked better in soft lighting but not so good if we needed to read Tyler's paperwork.

"Are you familiar with Indian cuisine?"

"Yes, well, no." My first instinct was to appear to Tyler as worldly and sophisticated, then in almost the same instant I remembered a date when I was just 16. My soon-to-be-ex boyfriend took me to a Mexican restaurant. Without realizing it I ordered the hottest thing on the menu and, with my girlish figure in mind, declined the rice that was normally served with it. I sweated like a horse and it took me an hour to choke down my meal. By the time I was done my hair was limp, my mascara unknowingly had run from my watery eyes and my dress was sticking damply to my back. There went that romance.

Tyler was looking a little puzzled at my response. "Why don't I order for both of us?"

"Good idea," I said.

"Do you like beer?"

Obviously my looks didn't shriek "Champagne."

"Yes."

"Then we'll both have Kingfisher beer and a pot of your fennel tea," he instructed the server. "We'll start with lamb kabobs and the cucumber, tomato and cilantro salad. For the main dish we'll have chicken biryani – medium heat. And please take your time. We don't want to be rushed."

Turning to me. "I hope you enjoy this. I spent six weeks traveling through India after college and I really came to love the food."

"It must be wonderful to travel. I've hardly been out of Mallowapple and I never went to college either." Since my attempt at dressing like someone that I'm not hadn't worked I figured it was better that I just be me. No point in pretending to be worldly or well-educated when I wasn't.

"College isn't all it's cracked up to be. Do you know how many highly educated people there are who can't find work in their field? I bet there are college grads who'd be glad to work for you right now."

"As a matter fact, there already is one." And next thing I knew I was telling Tyler how I'd always wanted to work with animals but hated school, so the idea of years of college just never appealed. I started as a dog walker, then people began to ask if I could help with other errands while they were at work or on vacation. Soon it was more than I could handle alone so I hired another person as an independent contractor. Now I had six contractors, all licensed, bonded and insured and operated a busy pet care and concierge service.

"What's next?"

"Eventually the pet boarding facility I mentioned to you before. Business is great but I've still got a lot of saving to do before I can afford a property."

"Well, I hope you'll come to me when you're ready."

I smiled wryly.

By the time our food arrived I'd learned that Tyler had taken over the family business when his dad took early retirement. He'd successfully expanded into commercial real estate and had more than 20 agents in his office. I wondered why he was bothering with our sale when he could easily hand it off to one of those other agents.

When I'd asked what he did for down time he'd looked puzzled. "Hobbies, sports, you know," I'd persisted.

"There's no time for play," was his response, and there I'd left it, thinking that explained his invitation to combine business with the necessary function of eating.

The meal was marvelous. Fragrant, moist and just spicy enough. While we ate Tyler told me he thought we could market the house for $300,000 to $350,000.

"That's terrific!"

"Before you get too excited, let me explain a couple of things. A house that large is actually harder to sell. You have more than 4000 square feet. Most people who are looking for something that size can afford a home that's new or completely modernized. And the outbuildings could be a plus – or not. They're not in bad shape but they do need some work and, again, a lot of people simply don't want to do that."

My elation was swiftly plummeting. "What do you suggest?"

"Stick with the original plan. Clean, paint and refinish the hardwood floors. That's still going to cost you about $15,000 but I can recommend people to do the work. On the other hand, if your mother would be happy in a condo then there are some newer properties, well under $100,000 and wheelchair accessible, that I can show you."

"OK, but what if the house doesn't sell?"

"It will sell. I'm giving you the worst-case scenario in the interests of full disclosure."

After that I felt rather deflated and Tyler obviously had no interest in me other than as a business prospect. *Why did I care? I hadn't even liked him at first.* But I did care. I was finding myself drawn more and more to him and I didn't like thinking of myself as the unrequited lover.

My mood picked up when we got dessert though. Something called Kulfi ice cream; amazingly light and sweet with my favorite pistachios and a hint of rose water. Yum!

Five

We were the last to leave the restaurant even though it was only nine. As we stepped outside, we realized why. Snow was falling heavily and it wouldn't be long before the roads were covered.

Tyler drove a Subaru Outback. It was turbocharged, all-wheel-drive and a smart choice for the sometimes rugged terrain where we lived and the bad weather we sometimes endured. We were parked a couple of blocks away in a covered area.

"I'll get the car and pick you up here," Tyler offered.

"No need. I can walk with you." *After all, I **was** wearing boots.*

As we neared the parking lot we heard raised voices coming from a nearby alley. Then very distinctly someone said, "Control that dog or I'll shoot him!"

That was enough for me. Without thinking I bolted round the corner yelling, "Don't shoot. Don't shoot."

Startled faces turned my way. A cop, legs wide with his gun in a two-fisted hold pointed toward an old man who had his arms round a large dog that was growling warningly at the cop.

The cop recovered first. "Get back, lady. This is police business."

I planted myself between the policeman and the dog. "Don't shoot. I can help."

"Lower that weapon!" It was Tyler, who'd followed me into the alley. His voice was so commanding that the officer looked confused. In a calmer tone Tyler continued, "I suggest you call for back-up and let's all behave reasonably about this."

"I don't know who the hell you think you are but you're interfering in a police matter." Waving his weapon at Tyler he ordered him to move over so that we were all bunched together. Then he did use his radio to call for help.

Behind me the old man was sobbing while still hugging his dog. He looked in his 70s though my guess was a hard life on the streets had aged him and he was probably closer to 60. And his dog was a she; a pitbull, more stocky than my Angel and not young, either. I hunkered down. "What happened?"

"He wants to take Elaine from me." *Elaine? Wonder who she was named after.* "She's all I've got. We've never been apart," and, in fits and starts, part of the story came out.

He'd rescued Elaine as a pup. Some kids had tied cans to her tail and were throwing fire crackers at her. Another pup was dead nearby with burns and cuts over its body. Rooster – that's the name he gave – chased the kids off. When he turned back to the pup, instead of trying to run off she came to him, cans and all dragging behind her. That kind of bond is not something that's ever shaken and, since then, Rooster and Elaine had wandered the country together, Rooster looking for work where he could, sometimes eating at soup kitchens and sneaking a few bites out to his friend. At night, sleeping wherever they could lay down together.

Apparently, the police officer, who looked like he'd be in his mid to late twenties and, I thought, was overly officious, had seen Rooster with Elaine checking dumpsters. He'd demanded Rooster's ID and address as well as Elaine's proof of ownership and rabies vaccination. When Rooster produced his identification and Elaine's vaccination record, the young cop told him he was still going to arrest him for vagrancy because he had no permanent address and Elaine would have to go to the pound. Rooster pleaded to be allowed to go on his way with his dog but the cop grabbed him to put him in handcuffs, at which point Elaine growled and the cop threatened to shoot her. Enter Tyler and myself.

At that moment the animal control vehicle pulled into the street. Tyler was standing in stony silence, his expression dark.

Rooster began to sob again. "Don't let them take her....please," he pleaded.

"I'm going to do everything I can to help," I promised him.

Five minutes later a heated argument was in force and I was at the center of it.

"Nobody has to go to jail and the dog doesn't have to go to the pound. How many times do I need to tell you, they can come home with me?"

"Lady, the old guy resisted arrest. He's going to jail and we're not leaving a dangerous dog on the streets."

"She's not dangerous," Rooster yelled and to prove it Elaine yawned, a dog's way of saying, "OK, time to lower the intensity level."

"There, you see," I shrieked, "How is that dangerous? Elaine is the sweetest thing ever." At which moment there was a loud blast on a horn.

"Who the hell is Elaine? Nobody told me another woman was involved."

We all turned. In our ire we hadn't even noticed that a second cruiser had arrived with the Animal Control vehicle. The man who spoke obviously had a few years' experience on the other cops and a good few pounds. *Maybe it was true about cops and doughnuts.*

"Rooney, explain!"

The first officer began to speak. When I tried to inject a few words the older cop glared at me. "Miss...?"

"Uh, Polly Parrett, and as I was saying..."

"You won't be saying anything unless you want to be arrested for obstruction. You'll get your turn later."

My jaw dropped. Then it dropped further when he turned to Tyler. "And what's your part in this, Breslin?" *They know each other?*

"We just happened on the scene, Sheriff," and briefly Tyler summed up the situation.

"Is that about right, Rooney?"

"Uh, yes sir, but ….."

"No buts. Here's what's going to happen. You're all coming down to the station to file a report. The dog is going to Animal Control."

"Noooo," wailed Rooster. "Run, Elaine. Go, go away." But the dog just cocked her head and looked confused.

"Rooster!" I said. "I promise I'll get her out and take care of her. She won't survive on the streets in this weather without you. It's better you let them take her for now."

"You promise you'll keep her safe?"

"I promise."

And with tears streaming down his face, Rooster lifted Elaine into the Animal Control van, whispering to her to be good, but as the van drove away we all heard Elaine's desperate howls.

Rooster was bundled into the back of a squad car while Tyler and I were instructed to follow them to the station. Once I was settled in the seat of the Subaru my righteous anger overcame me again. "I can't believe that Rooney was actually going to shoot Elaine."

Tyler hit the brakes and we skidded across the snow-slicked street almost hitting a fire hydrant 'til we ground to a stop against the curb.

"*You* can't believe he would shoot a *dog*? You nearly got shot yourself. What kind of a damn fool stunt was that to put yourself between a cop with an armed pistol – a nervous, inexperienced cop at that – and a snarling pitbull. Of all the stupid, dangerous ideas...... It's a damn good thing I called Sheriff Wisniewski."

"You called him?" I gasped. "Then you're responsible for Rooster and Elaine being split up."

"I'm responsible for preventing a bad situation from getting worse and maybe even for saving Rooster's and Elaine's lives."

Tyler's mood was beyond black by now and my own fury was redirected from Rooney to him.

"Saving their lives," I scoffed. "What are you? God?"

"Do you honestly think either of them could have survived outside tonight? Neither dog nor man are exactly young, and the temperature is going to drop into the teens."

"There are shelters!" I shot back.

"The shelters won't accept dogs and Rooster won't go if he can't take Elaine."

"Well, they could have come home with me."

Tyler sighed heavily and seemed to exhale his rage for he looked at me almost sadly. "You know it was already too late for that. And let's not get into the fact that you'd be taking in a total stranger, a vagrant you know nothing about, and a potentially dangerous animal."

My own anger had not yet deflated. "I'm not an idiot and I'm a good judge of character. Rooster is just a sad, old man who's been abandoned and ignored by cold-hearted people like you and Elaine is a sweet, loyal girl. They deserve better than this."

Tyler's lips tightened into a thin line and his jaw muscles clenched but he didn't respond. Instead, he rammed the car into gear and we fishtailed back onto the street and continued our way to the police station.

It took a couple of hours to give our statements and I wasn't allowed to see Rooster again. I wanted to reassure him about Elaine but was told I'd have to wait 'til the next day.

I was still mad as hell.

"Look young lady, I know you won't believe this right now, but I do sympathize. Thing is, I'd rather put a man behind bars for the night than be scraping up his dead body in the morning."

We were standing at the front entrance when Sheriff Wisniewski made this statement.

"My advice is to get home, get some rest and you'll see things differently in the morning."

Home? Rats! How was I going to get home?

"Do you have a number for a taxi?"

Wisniewski guffawed. "There aren't any taxis on a night like this."

"Well, what about a ride home in a squad car?"

He just looked at me.

"I'm taking you home." *Tyler!*

"I'd rather lie on a bed of nails and eat glass," I said in my best haughty dowager voice. To which Tyler responded by grabbing my elbow, dragging me out to the car and shoving me into the passenger's seat.

"Put your seat belt on," he hissed. "This is going to be a rough ride."

And it was. The road at times was completely hidden beneath the snow, which was rapidly freezing. A drive that normally took 20 minutes lasted well over an hour and it was only because of Tyler's skill at the wheel that we made it safely. Not that I would ever admit that.

Neither of us spoke the whole time. Not even when Tyler deposited me at my house then sped away, racing the wheels, the moment I closed the car door. And in that same moment I realized I'd left all the real estate paperwork in the file on the back seat.

Drat!

Six

Inside my head The Chipmunks were singing 'Pretty Woman.' It was really annoying and I couldn't get them to shut up. Then I opened my eyes. *Oh, right – the alarm.*

I'd set it early; I was on a mission today. I wanted to be at the county shelter when they opened at nine to spring Elaine from her prison and I had to stop on the way to check on Laurel and Hardy, a chatty pair of cockatiels whose pet parents were sunning themselves down in Florida.

My head felt like a bowling ball - I'd slept badly because I was so wired. As soon as I'd got in last night I'd called my mother to make sure she was OK. Thankfully the power was still on and she said everything was fine. I was keeping my fingers crossed that her aide would make it out there this morning.

With some difficulty I extricated myself from the bed. Ditto and the girls, Amber and Taz, my cats, didn't budge. Vinny and Coco looked up to see what the disturbance was then grunted and put their heads back down. Angel had her own bed – I rather envied her.

After a quick shower I dressed and headed outside to assess the situation. In the dark I could see that my van was iced-stuck to the driveway and the roads looked slippery as wet soap. In Maine we're used to rough weather and I figured with a little kitty litter I could rock the van out of the ice but I was concerned about the roads. The van is great for pets but not the most practical vehicle in this type of weather.

Mallowapple is a small town with a small budget so there was only one old snow plow to clear the streets; not that it would do much good with packed ice anyway. The pound was more than a 10 mile drive from my home but at least Laurel and Hardy were on the way.

By nine o'clock I'd made it to the shelter. I'd rushed to take care of my pets; the kitty litter had worked on the van; the cockatiels were in good shape and I'd crept along the roads at a max 20 miles an hour. I was feeling better about things as I reached to open the front door. Locked!

I checked my phone. It was just after nine so I began banging on the door 'til a harried-looking guy opened it.

"We're not open."

"It's after nine and I've come to pick up a dog."

"There's no-one here to help you. I'm just the overnight caretaker and my replacement should have been here an hour ago."

"Then I'll wait," I said, pushing past him.

"Suit yourself," he shrugged.

For the next hour I flicked through year-old copies of magazines that told me how to cook perfect pies, gave me pro tips for demolition and explained how I could sex up my love life. I was getting in to that last one when I heard, "Polly! What are you doing here on a day like this?"

Looking up I saw Dave Cartright behind the counter. We'd been at Mallowapple Junior High together; I used to help him with English grammar. He wasn't the brightest of the 'Mallowapples' but he was a sweet guy.

"Dave, I'm so glad it's you working today." And I told him Elaine's story.

As I finished speaking, he pulled out a file. When he looked inside his face creased into a deep frown.

"Polly, the dog was admitted as a dangerous animal. She can't be released. In fact, she's scheduled to be euthanized at noon."

"What! There's a mistake. Look again, please."

Dave shook his head. "I'm sorry, Polly."

"Wait. Who labeled her as dangerous?"

"Ummm. It's signed by Officer Rooney."

That scum!

"Dave, do you have the number for the county sheriff's office?"

Sheriff Wisniewski wasn't expected in 'til the afternoon. No amount of pleading with the desk sergeant could elicit a home number or any clue as to the sheriff's current whereabouts, nor was he listed in any phone directories. I was sick to my stomach with fear for Elaine. I figured the Sheriff was the only one with the authority to save her now and the last person who might be able to help me find him was also the last person I wanted to talk to – Tyler. For Elaine's sake I bit my tongue and dialed the phone.

"Hello, Polly." His voice was cold but at least he'd answered.

"They're going to kill Elaine," I blurted out and then promptly burst into tears.

Another agonizing hour passed with me pacing in the waiting room. After gulping out the story to Tyler he'd tersely told me would find the Sheriff, then hung up without further ceremony. Not another soul had entered the shelter; not surprising considering the weather and just fine by me - I didn't particularly want anyone to see me in my current state of angst.

"Polly!" Dave was back at the counter. "The Sheriff called." His face lit up. "He's rescinding the order to euthanize."

For a moment my heart stopped; I couldn't quite comprehend what I was hearing and then I burst into tears again – but this time, they were tears of relief. And of course, at that precise moment Tyler walked into the room. *Oh, God. He'll think I'm a weak crybaby. And I must look like hell.* I bawled even louder. Tyler looked astonished and Dave mutely held out a box of tissues. I grabbed a fistful and honked loudly into them. When I looked up I saw that Rooster was right behind Tyler. He was staring at me with an expression of utter fear and I realized he must think I was crying of grief.

"Rooster!" I sniffled. "It's OK, Elaine is safe."

"I'll go get her," Dave announced and while Rooster paced anxiously, I plopped weakly into a chair and Tyler stood stiffly to the side. None of us spoke.

A few minutes passed before we heard the scuffling sound of paws. Rooster stopped in his tracks and we all looked towards the door. As it opened, there stood Elaine. Man and dog gazed at each other for a split second and then all joy erupted. Elaine launched herself at Rooster. He went to his knees and held her to him, which wasn't easy because she was wriggling so much.

In my elation I forgot I was mad with Tyler. "How did you find the Sheriff?"

"He and my dad are both active in the VFW (Veterans of Foreign Wars)," he answered coolly. "I knew they had a board meeting this morning so I called down there."

"But what about Rooster? Did they just let him go?"

"He's out on bail."

"Bail? How could he get bail.....?" My voice faded away as realization dawned. "YOU paid his bail."

"Damn right he did." It was Rooster, standing with his hand on Elaine's head as she leaned against him.

Suddenly, I was starting to feel all warm and fuzzy toward Tyler again. "But what happens now? Where ....."

"Why don't we get out of here?" Tyler interrupted brusquely. "I still have a job to do and I need to get Rooster settled."

"Where are we going?" I asked.

"Tyler's letting us stay with him for a while," chimed in Rooster. "Fact is, if he hadn't offered us a place I'd still be in jail and my old girl would be stuck here." Turning to Tyler he continued, "And I'm going to find a way to pay you back, son. I've never taken charity in my life and I don't mean to start now."

Astonished, I looked at Tyler who was fidgeting uncomfortably. Damn, the man looked cute when he was embarrassed.

"And I'm grateful to you, young lady." Rooster turned to me. "Without you it might have been all over for Elaine. I'm really proud to know you." Now I was the one squirming with discomfort as I shook the hand he held out.

"Um, you're quite welcome," I mumbled. Then, more assertively, "And I'm coming with you. I want to hear everything that happened. In fact, why don't you and Elaine ride with me, Rooster? Then you can tell me your story." *And Tyler can't drive away leaving me behind.*

So off we went. Along the way I found out that Tyler had been at the jail with Rooster's bail when I phoned in panic. Tyler, he told me, didn't miss a beat. "He just took charge. Made some phone calls, made sure the right paperwork was done, then brought me over to the pound." *Hmm. Tyler's definitely decisive. I like that in a man.*

"He's also going to introduce me to his daddy and some others at the VFW. I'm a vet, too, you know - Vietnam. He says they can help people like me, but I'd be glad if they could just help me find a job."

"What sort of things can you do?"

"Well, in the air force I worked on the flight line. I'd been planning to go to college to study mechanical engineering when the war started. A lot of guys went on to college to avoid being drafted but I didn't think that was right, so I volunteered. Then a couple of years in, I got injured in a mortar attack. I was lucky, I just lost a bit of my jaw but they were able to rebuild it. Anyway, that was the end of the war for me. "

Rooster went on to tell me that his name was actually Washington Roosevelt. "I don't know what my parents were thinking, but at school the kids started calling me Rooster, and the name stuck." I also found out he married his high school sweetheart but started having flashbacks and, after a while, his young bride couldn't handle it and left. "I don't blame her," he said. "I could get pretty scary and apparently I struck out a couple of times and hurt her. I don't remember any of it but then I kept missing work at the local garage and they let me go. I was in my twenties and I didn't want to be a burden to my parents, so I hit the road."

"But that means you've been on the road for nearly forty years!"

"It hasn't been all bad. I'd get work here and there, stay in shelters, met some really good people along the way but then I got beaten up by a gang of teenagers and after that I couldn't use my left arm properly and I'll tell you, I was thinking it was time to end it all. That's when Elaine and I found each other. She needed me and I guess I needed her."

I was so appalled I simply didn't know what to say but by then we were pulling into Tyler's driveway. I'd rather expected him to be in the town center in a stylish condo. Instead, we were on the outskirts of Mallowapple and the home before us was a rustic-looking ranch with a wide front porch. I knew the area; I had clients nearby and all the homes were on five to 10 acre lots. Behind the house it was fenced and I wondered if Tyler had a dog. My question was immediately answered when a big brown dog came bouncing out of the house. He had huge, floppy ears, a somewhat crinkly face and the longest legs you can imagine.

Excitedly the dog greeted us all, including Elaine who sat placidly accepting his ministrations.

"His name's Frank," Tyler offered, "after an uncle he reminds us of. We think he's a great dane / bloodhound mix."

We?

I looked back toward the house. Standing in the open doorway a woman waved. A *young* woman. From this distance I couldn't really tell what she looked like but I was sure she must be pretty. How could I have been so stupid? It never occurred to me that Tyler was married.

"Let's go on in," said Tyler

"Actually, I think I'd better head back. I, uh, should check on my team and make sure there were no problems with the weather and stuff." I scuttled toward my car. "'Bye Rooster. I'll catch up with you later."

"Polly, wait!" It was Tyler. "Let me get that file for you so you can look it over with your mother."

I raised a hand in acknowledgement – I wasn't sure I could trust my voice – and got in the van. A few moments later Tyler returned with the papers. I wound the window down and took them, willing my hand not to shake and keeping my gaze averted.

"Are you OK? You don't look too good."

"I'm just cold." And to prove it, I cranked the heater as high as it would go.

"Let me drive you back home. In fact I'll drive your car and have Suzette follow in my car." *Suzette! Of course she'd also have a pretty name.*

"No! I'm all right." Then I made the mistake of looking directly at Tyler. The expression of genuine concern on his face was the final straw. I simply couldn't help myself and I burst into tears – again! Fumbling for the stick shift I managed to put it in reverse so I could back out onto the road.

"Polly. Polly! Stop! What's wrong?"

I could only shake my head as I came close to knocking down the mailbox, but I managed to turn the van and fishtail away, leaving Tyler standing alone in the driveway.

Liz Dodwell

Seven

Someone had pulled little wooly socks over my teeth in the night. At least, that's what it felt like. Talk about dry mouth. I'd made it back from Tyler's, checked with all my sitters to be sure everything was OK, taken care of my own 'zoo,' then poured myself a supersized glass of the only booze I had in the house – a bottle of homemade blackberry brandy, a gift from a client. It was sweet and syrupy and I'd cut it with root beer. Looking at the bottle this morning I saw I'd consumed more than half of it. No wonder my stomach was doing back flips, and the sugar rush it had given me kept me awake for most of the night. Serve me right for acting like an idiot over a guy I hardly knew.

I guzzled down about a gallon of water while the dogs took care of business in the back yard, and prayed none of my sitters would cancel out today. I had a really great crew but things sometimes happen. You know how it is.

Ditto was rubbing around my legs to remind me I had important things to do, like getting his breakfast.

"You'll have to wait a bit, buddy. I need a shower first."

I dragged my carcass to the bathroom, turned the water on hot and let it beat down over me. Of course, that's when the phone rang. I considered ignoring it but it could be a pet emergency. Swearing under my breath I turned off the water, wrapped a towel around me and raced to grab the thing before it stopped.

"Yes, this is Polly."

"Polly, it's Tyler." *What the hell?* It wasn't even seven yet.

"Is something wrong?" It couldn't be good if he was calling this early.

"Rooster's been arrested."

The shock silenced me. Had I heard right? That didn't make sense.

"Polly! Polly, are you there?"

"Did you say Rooster was arrested?"

"The police turned up late last night. They had an arrest warrant for murder."

I simply didn't know what to say. Finally I managed to blurt out, "Murder. But who was killed?"

"A body was found in one of the dumpsters where we found Rooster. As far as I know it hasn't been identified."

"This is insane. Where's Rooster now? Why didn't you call me when this happened?" "When was the body found?" I knew I was babbling but I couldn't seem to stop. Then another thought hit me. "What about Elaine?"

"Elaine is still at my house; she's fine. I did call you, three times, and you have three messages on your voicemail that you obviously haven't checked yet." *Oops, there I go with my big mouth again.* "The body was found late yesterday afternoon, when the trash was being picked up. And Rooster is being held at the sheriff's department until a vehicle can get through to take him to county jail."

"What can we do?" Indignation was beginning to rise in me. "We can't let him be railroaded like this."

"Polly," Tyler's voice was weary, "I've been up all night, I'm still at the station and there's nothing else I can do right now. I'm going home to get some sleep and then I'll be able to think more clearly."

"You can't just abandon Rooster like that."

I heard a sharp intake of breath. "Do you *never* stop? Where were *you* all night? Tucked up in bed and fast asleep, I suppose. And is it at all conceivable that you could believe Rooster just might be guilty? Keep in mind we really don't know him, and he *was* hanging round the dumpster where the body was found."

No, it wasn't conceivable that Rooster was a cold-blooded killer but I bit back the sharp retort I was about to make as I heard my mother's voice in my head, *Once spoken, can't be mended.* Tyler didn't deserve my sharp tongue. Without him Elaine would be dead and it's true, he was there for Rooster last night while I was crying in my blackberry brandy.

"Tyler, I'm sorry. This has been such a shock I'm not thinking clearly. Look, I have a few visits to make this morning. Could we meet later and perhaps between us we can work something out? And let me know if you need help with Elaine. I can go and walk her or even keep her with me."

"We can get together at my office, if that's OK with you? I've already left a message for my attorney so I should have something from him by then. And don't worry about Elaine, my sister will look after her."

Sister?

"Uh, that would be Suzette, is it?"

"Sure. She was disappointed you didn't stay yesterday. She wanted to meet you."

"Oh, well, another time." Suddenly, I was feeling a whole lot better.

Eight

We were in the conference room at Tyler's realty office. On the speakerphone Tyler's attorney was talking. "I've contacted Zill Granger and he's agreed to talk with Rooster, but don't assume that means he'll take the case."

"Who's Zill Granger?" I wanted to know.

"He's the best criminal defense attorney in these parts; I only do corporate. Granger will take a look at the evidence and then contact you later. And, Tyler, you do know Granger is pretty expensive?"

"Let me worry about that."

I gave Tyler a grateful look. He was turning out to be a real prince.

"OK. Just wanted to give you a heads-up. I can also tell you that Rooster will be moved this afternoon at two and Granger will meet with him at county."

"Any word on the murder victim?"

"As I'm not the attorney of record the authorities wouldn't give me anything more. You'll have to wait on Granger."

The lack of information was really frustrating me. "When will we be able to see Rooster?"

"Again, I don't know. My advice is to let Granger do what he does best and then you'll be able to make better-informed decisions."

"Right, thanks Fred." Tyler was bringing the conversation to a close. "I appreciate you getting on this so quickly. And send me your bill personally, not to the company."

"It's on me. Your family has done me enough favors over the years and this was nothing much."

With that, we hung up.

Vinny was sitting in my lap while I absent-mindedly scratched his head. Whenever I could I brought the dogs with me and it hadn't occurred to me until I got to Tyler's office that it might not be a good idea. It was too cold to leave them in the van but Tyler had no problem with me bringing them in. In fact, he said he sometimes brought his own dog to work. He'd even lifted Coco up and was now cradling her like a baby, which she absolutely loves.

"Look," I said, "you shouldn't have to foot the bill for a lawyer. I don't have much but I can chip in something." It would have to be an advance on my credit card but I didn't mention that.

Tyler's mouth raised in a crooked smile. "Let's just see how it goes. Meanwhile, I have a business to run and there's nothing else we can do for Rooster right now."

I can take a hint when I have to, and I really needed to get out and check on my mother. The aide hadn't been able to make it out there this morning so mom had to get dressed as best she could. By now she'd probably be in a really foul mood. With luck the dogs would cheer her up. It's hard to be mad when three lovable mutts act like they missed you more than anything in the world.

The drive took longer than usual with the roads still really slick. I took the opportunity to check in with all my crew and was relieved to hear no problems. By the time I pulled up to the house it was nearly two and I was starving. I hadn't felt well enough to eat breakfast and had skipped lunch, too.

The dogs leapt from the van in joyous abandon and bounded through the snow drifts. It would do them good to run around for a while so I steeled myself to deal with my mother and stepped into the house.

Mom was at the window with Cappy on her lap, and she was laughing! I'd practically forgotten that sound; it had been so long since I'd heard it.

"Mom?"

"Come and look. Vinny and Coco are being stealth dogs."

Puzzled, I looked outside and realized what she found so funny. Angel was looking for the two white poodles, but they'd figured out all they had to do was stay still, cloaked in the snow, and she couldn't see them. In fact, if Mom hadn't pointed out the two pairs of eyes peeking through the drifts I would never had known they were there. I laughed with her and it felt good for once to be sharing a happy moment. And before long I found myself telling her about Rooster and Elaine, and Tyler's part in the affair and even about my confused feelings for him.

"Tyler is a nice young man. I knew it the first time I saw him. And he's right about this Rooster character; you really don't know him at all. Remember, a man has been murdered."

"Mom, I'm telling you, Rooster is a good guy. Anyone who can love a dog the way he loves Elaine couldn't be a killer."

"Polly, even some of the worst criminals have loving relationships with pets. I'm not saying Rooster is a criminal, but I am asking you to keep an open mind. You've done all you can for now so, please, let the police and the attorney handle things."

There was no way I was going to let the police bungle things up and I was about to say so, but the look of concern on my mother's face made me swallow the words and I meekly agreed, while keeping my fingers crossed behind my back. My mother knows me well, though, and she sighed deeply and said, "Well, at least promise you'll be very careful."

Grinning, I kissed her on the cheek and for the next hour took care of a few chores around the house, while the dogs came in and settled themselves round the wood stove in the kitchen. When I was ready to leave I found Mom again at the window.

"I'll be off now."

She turned and gave a wistful smile. "I was remembering how much I loved Christmas here when you and the boys were little. We'd have lights around the porch and in the trees outside, and your dad would climb up on the roof and stamp around while I jingled bells in the living room, and...."

"…and we were quite, quite sure it was Santa."

"It was lovely, wasn't it? To gather pine cones and branches and wrap them in big, red bows to decorate the house. I'll miss all that when I have to leave here."

"But we haven't celebrated Christmas here in years."

Mom sighed. "It still always meant so much to look at the mantle over the fireplace and remember the stockings hanging there. And in my mind I can see you, when you were five, sitting by the rocking chair as you unwrapped that stuffed toy rabbit with the red hat and blue bow tie."

"Mr. Beanie," I said. *And I still had him.* "But I so wanted a real bunny."

"Well, I think you've made up for it since then."

I smiled. "Yes, I have."

Liz Dodwell

Nine

Mom's words stayed with me as I drove away later. The farmhouse had been a wonderland of merriment for many Christmases. As a small child I'd been awestruck by the miracle of presents under the tree. In later years it was the gathering of our happy family wrapped in love for each other that seemed miraculous. By the time I was twenty – and Mom was in a wheelchair - it was a miracle if we could spend Christmas day together without Mom's self-pitying absorption dragging us all down to a level of petty bickering.

I made up my mind that I would persuade my brothers to help me bring the magic back home for one last Christmas. We had nearly three weeks to get things together and all the old decorations were still up in the attic. Maybe it would help lift Mom's spirits.

Feeling pretty festive myself, I hummed along to the seasonal tunes playing on the radio as I drove. There was one quick stop I needed to make – my nemesis, Pookie Pie. Pookie was a large, fluffy gray feline of indeterminate origin and sociopathic tendencies. His owner, Bob, doted on him and believed him to be the sweetest creature in all the world. If that was the case, then Pookie used up all his sweetness on his loving pet-parent and saved his ugly, sourpuss self for the rest of us.

Once a week, Bob, a retired librarian, took a day-trip out of town to visit his ailing sister. Truth to tell, Pookie didn't need a visit, but it made the over-anxious Bob happier to know his beloved was being checked on. I didn't think I should inflict 'his nastiness' on any of my crew, so I always took care of Pookie myself.

I trotted up to the front door, key in hand, unlocked it and pushed it inward. A one-inch gap opened before the door came to a jarring stop. *What the…?*

Tentatively I pushed a little harder. Nothing. I put my eye to the gap and swore. *Pookie!*

Bob had an antique hall stand just inside the doorway. It had drawers in it. One of the drawers was open and blocking the doorway. Sitting in the open drawer was Pookie.

Honestly, I swear the bloody cat knows when I'm coming. How he got the drawer open I had no idea. The stand was mahogany and the drawer was heavy. I just had to figure how to get it closed.

It was freezing cold so I jumped back in the van for a while and turned on the heat. The dogs merely wagged their tails at me while I wondered if I could get my hand far enough through the crack in the door to ease the drawer closed, finger over finger. Nothing else was coming to me so I figured I'd give it a try.

Back at the door I peeked in again. Pookie was still sitting there. "Shoo! Sssst! Yip!" I made a variety of noises and banged on the door to get him to move. He weighed more than twenty pounds, for cripe's sake. He casually lifted a paw and began washing it.

"You……!" Relax Polly. He's just a cat.

Forcing my left hand through the gap I got two fingers under the drawer and attempted to lift and close it a little. Have you ever tried lifting thirty pounds with two fingers? I made about a quarter-inch headway when there was sharp sting in my forefinger. With a gasp I yanked my hand out. That little so and so had clawed me! Sucking the blood and nursing my wounded dignity at being bested by a cat, I trotted back to the van to look for an adhesive bandage.

Now what?

I hated to admit defeat and call Bob. Not that I wanted Pookie on my roster but I didn't want to let Bob down, either; his visits to his sister were really important to him. With a sigh I headed back to the door and banged and yelled again, to no avail. I broke a twig off a bush and tried to shove it through the door to poke him. The twig snapped, Pookie looked me right in the eye, yawned and curled up in the drawer, his back to me.

"Aaaaaargh!" I screamed aloud.

"Step back slowly, turn around and keep your hands where I can see them."

The voice scared the bejeezus out of me, so of course I jumped around with arms in a defensive position, only to see Officer Rooney before me, legs apart and hand on his holstered gun.

"Holy cow, what are you doing?" My heart was racing.

"I'm the one who should be asking that question."

"I come every week to take care of Bob's, Mr. Stanton's, cat. Why are you here? Has something happened to Bob?" A sense of alarm was beginning to set in.

Rooney ignored my questions. "Looks to me as if you were trying to break in. All that banging and shouting."

Moron. "If I was trying to break in would I make a lot of noise?" I grit my teeth, took a calming breath and spoke slowly. "Look, I'm a pet-sitter. I take care of pets. Here are the house keys." I held them up. "The door is stuck because the cat opened a drawer and I was yelling to get him to move."

Rooney's face showed disbelief and I had to admit, even to myself that sounded pretty strange. Thankfully, Bob chose that moment to pull into the driveway. Ignoring Rooney, he came straight to me. "Pookie?"

"Everything's fine, Bob. Pookie's up to his tricks; he's blocked me from getting in."

Bob laughed out loud when he heard the story. "That's my Pookums. I should have let you know there's a kitchen door key hidden in the back." *If only.*

Officer Pinhead was dismissed, though not before he got in a last word about disturbing the peace, and Bob and I went into the house. Pookie immediately morphed into a sweet, lovable creature while Bob explained he'd tried to call to tell me he'd be home early. "It kept going straight to your voicemail. You didn't need to come, Polly. I'm sorry." I pulled out my cell and looked at it. The battery was dead. *Oh, well.*

Ten

Back in my car I plugged in the phone and saw there was a message from Tyler. Granger was taking the case. *Yes!*

Of course, I called Tyler back straight away. Turned out Granger not only felt he could help Rooster, he was taking the case pro bono. He'd looked into Roosters background and was impressed with his service and disgusted that he'd pretty much been abandoned afterwards.

"Granger is an ex JAG lawyer."

"JAG. What's that?"

"Judge Advocate General's Corps. It's the legal branch of the military," Tyler explained, "so he has a soft spot for veterans."

"That's terrific. When can we visit Rooster?"

I heard Tyler take a deep breath. "We can't." Shocked, I waited for more. "Only family members are allowed."

"That's bull. Rooster doesn't have any family. Can't we just say we're his niece and nephew or something?"

"It wouldn't work. There's a vetting process, which takes weeks anyway. Look, I'm as bummed as you about this. Why don't we get together and I'll fill you in on everything? There's something else I want to talk to you about as well." *Like, maybe, I'm crazy about you?* "Are you home?"

"On the way."

"I'm only a few minutes from your place. I'll meet you there."

Not again. Here I was in grungy old dog-walking duds, without a scrap of make-up on. I sighed. I was never going to make a good impression on the man.

By the time I got home Tyler was already there. As we stepped inside I glanced around and breathed an inward sigh of relief – it didn't look so bad after all. As long as he didn't go in the bathroom where I had freshly washed bras and panties hanging over the shower rod it would be OK.

"Do you mind if I use your bathroom?"

Oh no! "Um, if you can wait just a couple minutes, I'm pretty desperate myself." *And that's no lie.* Not waiting for a response I dashed in the room and slammed the door shut. Snatching the undies down I looked wildly around for a hiding place. The medicine cabinet was the only thing with a door and it was too small. I'd have to stuff everything behind the towels on the shelf.

Reasonably satisfied my intimates were out of sight, I fluffed my hair, groaned at the bags under my eyes and casually exited.

While Tyler did his thing I cleared some space at the dining table, which doubled as my desk, and did my best to find a pose that said sexy, yet confident but was probably more desperate and pathetic. None of that mattered anyway when Tyler came out holding my best pink bra on his finger. "I needed a towel........uh..." He couldn't say any more because he was obviously trying really hard not to laugh. With delicate precision I removed the garment from his hand, headed into the bedroom and threw it down, stuffing my hand into my mouth and giving a silent scream. That done, I plastered a smile on my face, went back to the table and resumed my pseudo-sexy pose. "So what did you want to talk about?"

Immediately, Tyler became serious.

"Elaine isn't doing so well. She won't eat and I'm worried about her. She's really pining for Rooster."

"Damn, we should have expected that. Is she at least drinking water?"

"She just lays around and shows no interest in anything. Suzette even cooked chicken for her but she didn't give it a look."

"OK, let's not panic. Here's what to do. We need an item of clothing or something with Rooster's scent on it that we can give her. Without alarming Rooster, let's find out what her favorite food is. I assume we can still talk to him on the phone?" Tyler nodded. "It may be she's never liked chicken."

"A dog that doesn't like chicken!"

"You'd be surprised. Three of my cats won't touch it; they only want cheap commercial cat food."

Tyler looked skeptical.

"How many kids do you know who would eat spinach and fish rather than a Happy Meal?"

The light bulb went on. "Oh, yeah," Tyler said.

Soon we had a plan of action. Tyler would ask the lawyer to bring us a used shirt from Rooster so Elaine could have something imprinted with his scent. Meanwhile, we'd offer hot dogs – that always worked with my gang. For good measure, I'd give her some fluids. I always kept an emergency

IV bag on hand, with a boost of B vitamins. "When do you want to do this?"

"Now would be good."

We agreed to ride together then Tyler would bring me home later. Snow was falling again and his Subaru would handle it better than my van.

We entered his house through the kitchen door and were met by the aroma of fresh baked bread. A slender young woman was chopping vegetables at a butcher block counter. Her hands moved with speed and precision and when she saw us she wiped them down the front of a cute, vintage-style striped apron. She smiled and stepped toward me, hands out in welcome. "You're Polly. Oh, I'm so delighted to meet you at last."

I really felt she meant it, and before I knew what was happening she put her arms around me and gave me a sisterly hug.

"Tyler talks so much about you." *He does?* I wasn't sure if that was good or bad, but I willingly allowed myself to be drawn into the warmth of Suzette's personality.

"I expect you're here for Elaine." She gestured toward the corner where Elaine lay on the floor, showing no interest in us whatsoever. "We got her a big, plush doggy bed but she won't use it."

"She's spent most of her life sleeping on the ground. Eventually she'll try the bed and then I bet she won't want to get out." I hoped I knew what I was talking about. "Anyway, let me see what I can do with her."

I went to her and crooned over her for a while. She gave me a look and the slightest flick of her tail, which I took as a good sign. Perhaps she remembered me. She was definitely a little dehydrated, though, so I hooked up the IV and allowed the fluids to do their work. "Let's try her with some hot dog."

Suzette handed me a bag. "They're all beef."

I broke off a piece and waved it under Elaine's nose, then touched it to her lips. She instinctively licked her mouth so I offered the piece to her. She nosed it a little and licked it, then lay her head down again with a sigh.

"Oh, I thought she was going to eat it." Suzette was disappointed while, Frank, Tyler's mutt, looked expectantly at me, so I tossed the piece to him.

"Don't feel too bad," I said to Suzette, "she showed some interest and that's encouraging. I don't suppose you have any peanut butter, do you?"

Tyler, who'd been standing back reached into a cupboard and brought out a jar. "Here."

"Keep it for later. It might stress her if we try and force anything else on her right now. Give her a couple of hours then put a little on her nose. She'll automatically lick it off and, with luck, it will spark her appetite."

"You can do that after dinner. You're staying to have spaghetti with us." *I love spaghetti.*

I mumbled all the usual things about not wanting to be a bother, while my taste buds were screaming, 'Shut up, you idiot.' Thankfully, Suzette was insistent, and I spent a truly pleasant evening with brother and sister. They were obviously very close.

"When he heard the snow storm was heading our way, Tyler insisted I come and stay with him. He seems to think I'm not capable of looking after myself." She smiled fondly at him.

"Hey, that's what big brothers are supposed to do."

"The good thing is," Suzette explained with an innocent look on her face, "then I get to meet the women he likes."

I felt my cheeks begin to burn and Tyler hurriedly changed the subject by telling me that Suzette also worked for the family business, handling the finances and other paperwork.

"Most of the time I'm able to work from home," she said. "In fact, as long as I have my laptop and cell phone I'm good to go anywhere."

Suzette wanted to know about my business. I had plenty of funny stories to tell and we shared a good few laughs before the meal was over.

I managed to get Elaine to lick a couple of blobs of peanut butter from her nose, but she would not be persuaded to eat anything else. At the end of the evening, though, she stood up and began to whine, then pace around in an agitated manner.

"What's wrong?" Suzette was alarmed.

"Probably the IV fluids are making her want to pee," I said. "I'll put her on a lead and take her out."

"I'll do it." Tyler stood. "I need to let Frank out as well."

"I'm quite impressed that Elaine would ask to go out," Suzette said. "I wouldn't have thought she'd be house-trained."

"More likely it's imprinted on her to go in the outdoors. She just wants to do things the way she's always done them." *And she is a really good girl.*

By the time Tyler drove me back there was another inch of snow on the ground: soft vanilla cream on top of hot chocolate popped into my mind. Mallowapple residents took the holidays seriously and many houses were alive with strands of colored lights, chubby snowmen in the front yards and a good few Santas hanging out of chimneys. It was enough to make any cynic feel optimistic. If you're a Christmas lover, like me, you can believe that wishes *will* come true. So, silently, I made a wish that Rooster and Elaine would be together again by Christmas day.

Tyler insisted on walking me to the door. I'd like to think it's because I inspired his gentlemanly spirit, but I suspect it's because he was afraid I'd fall and hurt myself and then he'd be stuck with me for a while. Anyway, at the door he let go my arm and I cursed myself for not hanging mistletoe from the lintel. So I was surprised and excited when he leaned toward me – *he's going to kiss me!* – and gave me a chaste kiss on the cheek. *Rats!*

Liz Dodwell

Eleven

The next morning was business as usual. One of my crew had slipped on ice and hurt her elbow. She was on the way to get it X-rayed; meanwhile, I'd have to pick up her visits.

I was out the door at 7.30. At 12.30, weary and very hungry – there had been no time for breakfast – I found a parking spot near Bennie's Diner and trudged inside. The diner was an institution, famous for its Mallowapple meatloaf. As far as I knew, there was actually no apple in the meatloaf, nor was there a Bennie. In fact, no-one knew who Bennie was. The current proprietress of the establishment was Nita, a middle-aged, motherly type who knew more about town gossip than the women who hung out at the Combing Attractions hair salon.

Bennie's always did a steady business but I got lucky and scored an empty window booth. The diner was only a few doors from the Indian restaurant where Tyler and I had eaten on the night we met Rooster, which meant it was also close to where the body had been found.

Nita herself came to get my order.

"Well, hi, hon. How ya doing? I hear you got yourself mixed up in a murder. What happened?"

There's nothing subtle about Nita's insatiable desire for scandal. I tried to deflect her interest.

"I'm really in a rush, Nita. Can I get my order in and then maybe we can chat if I have time?"

"I already ordered the meatloaf for you, and Cindy's bringing coffee. We'll have a few minutes before your meal comes out."

Wow, the woman has this down to a fine art. I caved and gave her a very abbreviated version of events, by which time the food arrived and I stuffed my mouth so I couldn't talk any more. Nita slid from the booth, then paused.

"You know, the guy was in here just before it happened.

I practically spit the food out. "Sit back down," I spluttered. "You mean the victim?"

"Don Hardwicke? Yeah."

"How do you know his name?"

"That new officer; Rooney. He's a strange one, he is. Acts like he's Wyatt Earp or something. He was in here, too, that night."

My head was spinning. "Back up, Nita, and start from the beginning."

She slid back into the booth and I learned that Rooney had a thing for Cindy, the waitress, who couldn't stand him. *Smart girl.* Trying to impress her, he'd given her his version of the incident, in which he single-handedly captured a dangerous criminal, *the lying scumbag*, and had let slip Hardwicke's name.

"Did he say anything else about the victim?"

"No, but I chatted with the man a bit myself." *Of course you did, bless you.* "He was a nice young man. Said he was a giftware and décor salesman. He was just passing through Mallowapple but the roads were so bad he decided it would be safer to stay the night. Do you believe it? He thought he'd be safe and he ends up dead. Poor man."

"Did you tell the sheriff this?"

"Course I did. Not about the name, though. I didn't know that 'til after I spoke to the sheriff."

"Was there anything else that happened? Anything unusual?"

"Now that you mention it, he left all of a sudden. Hadn't even finished his dinner; just threw money on the table and hurried out. I wouldn't have noticed 'cept Cindy was saying good riddance that Rooney was out the door.... "

"Whoa, whoa! Rooney was here, too?"

"That's right. He just picked up a coffee to go. I dealt with him myself so he wouldn't have a chance to bother her and was watching him walk out the door and that's when Hardwicke got up and left."

"Did they notice each other – Rooney and Hardwicke?"

"I couldn't say, hon."

"Well, what time was it?"

"I don't know exactly, but it must have been about twenty minutes before the hullaballoo in the alley."

I asked Cindy a few questions, hoping she might have more to add, but that was that.

I needed to share this with Tyler, so I gave Nita a big hug. "Don't ever change anything about yourself." Startled, she laughed, "Why ever would I?"

Back in my van I hit speed dial. *OK, so I have Tyler on speed dial; it's no big deal.*

"I was just about to call you," he answered.

Without waiting to hear why, I blurted out my news.

"Hmm, that's pretty interesting." That wasn't exactly the level of excitement I was hoping to hear.

"This opens up a whole lot of questions"

"I get that," he said, "but before we discuss it, let me tell you why I was going to call."

Oh, right. I forgot he had news as well.

"Zill Granger stopped by with a sweater and jeans from Rooster, so I'm on the way home with them now. Elaine drank a little water this morning but still wouldn't eat, so let's hope this does the trick.

"Granger also arranged for Rooster to call at three this afternoon. Can you be available?"

It was already nearly two and I had a date with Mutz von Kuckenschutz, a young and energetic german shepherd who required an hour-long walk.

"No problem; we can do a three-way call," Tyler said. "I'll call you as soon as I have Rooster on the line."

"Works for me," I replied.

"Think about what you want to ask or say. Rooster is only allowed 15 minutes and we don't want to waste the time."

A little before the appointed hour, as I was settling Mutz back in his house, my phone rang. Expecting Rooster to be on the line I answered with a cheerful "Hey, Rooster."

"Polly, it's only me." *Tyler.* "I want to give you some good news quickly – Elaine ate some chicken. Your idea worked, Polly. She got Rooster's scent from the clothes and her tail started wagging immediately. Now we don't have to pretend everything's alright."

"That's wonderful. I'm so relieved."

"Me, too. Now hang up; Rooster should be calling any moment."

Liz Dodwell

Twelve

When the phone rang again a few minutes later, it was with a genuinely happy voice that I answered. Rooster, naturally, wanted to know all about Elaine, and Tyler and I gladly told him all was well.

"She's a sweetheart," I said. "You've nothing to worry about."

"How do you like Zill Granger?" Tyler switched gears, conscious of the clock.

"He's a fine man. I don't know how I'm ever going to repay you all for your help but I promise I'll find a way."

We mumbled things like, 'no need' and 'glad to,' then asked a few questions in hopes Rooster might remember something helpful, but there was nothing new. He'd never heard of Donald Hardwicke, never been in Mallowapple before, hadn't seen or heard anything unusual. "Except when Elaine growled," he added.

"What do you mean?" Tyler and I asked simultaneously.

"She doesn't have a mean bone in her body, but she growled at the officer."

"He was being aggressive toward you, so I wouldn't think that's so odd," I said.

"That's not it. She started growling before he ever said a word or pulled his gun. It's just not like her.

Liz Dodwell

"Look, they're telling me I've got to go. Hug Elaine for me and tell her I love her." He started to choke up. "And thank you both, again. Thank you, thank….."

Rooster's voice cut off and for a moment there was silence.

"Polly! Are you still there?"

"I'm here. I'm just not sure what to say. This is all so wrong."

"Don't lose faith. Granger says all the evidence is circumstantial. There's nothing to tie Rooster to the body; no prints, no DNA."

I sighed. "That's only what I expected, but it doesn't get Rooster his freedom yet."

Thirteen

For the next few days things hummed along much as usual. My one sitter was still out. I was able to spread her visits amongst the rest of my crew except for Tiddles, who needed three visits a day, five days a week.

You might guess how Tiddles got her name. She was a lovely long-haired dachshund, and a puppy mill rescue. They're notoriously hard to house train, but whenever Tiddles got excited or upset, well, she just couldn't contain herself.

Tiddles and her pet parents were fairly new clients and, frankly, I was having a harder time training them than their dog. Try getting two boisterous young boys to come through the door slowly and calmly and ignore their pup for a while. The mother wasn't much better. She would talk to the pooch in a high-pitched baby voice – not that there's anything wrong with that, I do it all the time – but it also triggered Tiddles tiddles. The good news was they loved their little pup and were committed to giving her a happy life.

The roads had all been cleared and I was making my regular visits out to see Mom. She was still in a nostalgic mood, and I'd spoken to my brothers who both agreed it would be a great idea to plan one last family Christmas at the old home.

Suzette had got into the habit of phoning each day to give me updates on Elaine. I was realizing that was indicative of her thoughtful, generous nature. She was still at Tyler's and had issued a standing invitation to come over any time, but I'd just been too busy.

During one call she had a request. Tyler was driving to Bangor on business the next day, and Suzette wanted to go with him and do some Christmas shopping. Frank would be fine on his own, he could let himself out through the doggy door, but she wasn't comfortable leaving Elaine. Would I take her?

Of course, I was delighted. I had a full schedule, but Elaine could ride along for the day with me.

So the following morning, Tyler and Suzette dropped Elaine off at my house on their way out of town. Tyler was wearing the suit he'd worn when he first came to Mom's house - sans dog hair - and this time with a light gray shirt and skinny tie in a cornflower blue paisley pattern. He looked so sizzling hot he practically melted the ice off the doorstep.

We made arrangements for the pair to collect Elaine when they got back, said our goodbyes and I watched as Tyler pulled away, wishing I could be the kind of arresting beauty who probably caught his eye.

I'd already walked Angel, Vinny and Coco so I bundled Elaine into the van and off we went. My dogs are not allowed in the front seat but I made an exception for Elaine and let her sit beside me, thinking she might not like the van because driving was a pretty new experience for her. I needn't have worried. She sat up, gazing with some apparent interest at the passing scenery. Whenever I made a stop, she waited placidly for me.

By mid-morning, I figured I'd better give her a quick walk. We stopped in the town center, where there was a small park. I'd put Elaine into a harness that would be more secure than a collar. As if she understood that, she'd licked my hand and wagged her tail.

So, there we were ambling around, Elaine sniffing the grass and me thinking she must be just about the sweetest dog in the world. She finally found a spot that suited her 'business' and I was just reaching for a doggy bag when she belied my earlier thought with a low, insistent growl.

"You'd better be planning to pick that up."

By now I knew that voice – Rooney. Wordlessly, I turned while pulling my hand from my pocket with one of the pink, paw-print-branded baggies that I used for pick-up duty.

Putting on the kind of syrupy voice that really irritates people, I held up the bag. "Perhaps you'd like to do the honors."

Rooney's eyes narrowed and he stepped toward me, at which point sweet Elaine morphed into mean dog. She stood stiffly, head forward and ears back, her muzzle wrinkled to expose her teeth, a deep snarl in her throat. It halted Rooney in his tracks immediately.

"That's it. I'm calling this in and getting animal rescue to come and pick that beast up."

For a few beats I stopped breathing, then a flood of anger surged in me. I reached for my phone and started scrolling through the contacts.

"What are you doing?"

"I'm calling Sheriff Wisniewski to report you for threatening me, then I'm calling Zill Granger, my attorney."

Whether Rooney was more afraid of the sheriff or the lawyer I don't know, but my ploy had him backing off faster than a scalded cat.

"Hold up a minute. Let's not be hasty." He held his hands palms forward in a submissive gesture.

"Hasty," I retorted, "it's not *me* being hasty."

"OK, maybe I jumped the gun." *There's a truism for you.* "But I'm an officer of the law and it's my job to keep the town safe and you can't deny she was aggressive to me."

"And you can't deny you were threatening towards me about scooping poop. Besides, you're the only one Elaine's ever growled at." *Which shows really good taste.* I didn't add that last bit, of course.

"Maybe I'll let it go this time."

"This time? Are you saying there'll be a next time? Are you stalking me, Rooney?"

I must have hit a nerve, the man visibly paled.

"Don't be absurd. I'm an officer…"

"Of the law. Yeah, yeah, so I heard." I was on a roll now and ready to give him a real tongue-lashing, but in an effort to save some dignity he actually pretended to get a call over the radio. It was laughable. We both knew that he knew that I knew the call wasn't real (did you get that?), but I decided it was wiser to go along with the hoax and just get rid of him.

"You'd better go where you're needed, Rooney."

He had to throw a few last words at me as he stalked off. "I won't forget this, Miss pet-sitter." And he wasn't saying it in an endearing sort of way.

Even though I had no undies hanging in the bathroom, I was relieved when Tyler and Suzette declined my offer to come in when they arrived to collect Elaine. Frankly, I was embarrassed for Suzette to see what a sloppy housekeeper I was, when she could have been the next Martha Stewart.

"I do have some news for you, though," I said, to which Suzette immediately suggested I come with them.

"Thanks, but I have to deal with payroll tonight or I won't have anyone working for me." Then to Tyler I said, "Call me later if you have time."

I gave Elaine a great big hug, said my goodbyes and girded my loins for paperwork.

A big glass of wine was at my side; my reward for completing my fiscal duties. I was about to take a sip when Tyler phoned. I launched into an account of my confrontation with Rooney. In the telling, some of my agitation came back but I didn't realize it until Tyler interrupted.

"Calm down, Polly. Take a deep breath and another sip of wine."

"How do you know I'm drinking wine?"

"I saw a bottle on the table when you brought Elaine to the door."

I laughed. "OK, Sherlock, now tell me who killed Donald Hardwicke."

"That I can't do, yet, but I can tell you his wife is in town."

"Really?"

"My dad told me. You remember he and the sheriff are pals: they had a card game last night and Wisniewski said the wife is at the C'mon Inn with her father. They had to identify the body and apparently are staying a few more days."

"Hmmm. I wonder if they'd talk to us."

"I'm not sure how it would help," Tyler said. "I suppose it's worth a try, though."

So we agreed to meet at the inn the following morning, then I went back to my thoughts and my wine.

Fourteen

The text read, 'Can't make it, can you go it alone?' I was already at the door of the C'mon Inn when Tyler's message came through. Having never conducted an interview in a murder investigation before I was a little unnerved at being in sole charge, but I certainly wasn't going to let Tyler know that. I replied, 'No problem.'

Hattie Pan was the proprietress of the inn, a tall, angular woman, brittle as old bones. Her late husband had been the jovial side of the partnership, but despite her lack of congeniality she ran a clean and charming establishment and had a steady business. She also had a pair of Siamese named Chatty and Kathy, with whom I was on speaking terms as their caregiver when Hattie visited her family in Ohio once a year.

"Hi, Hattie." I leaned casually against the reception desk as Hattie responded to the dinging of the bell.

"Oh, it's you," spoken with a nasal twang while looking down said nose.

"I'm looking for Mrs. Hardwicke. Can you give me her room number?"

"And just why would you want to see her, Polly Parrett? She doesn't have any pets with her."

"How are *your* little darlings, by the way?"

In an instant her demeanor softened and she began to prattle on about Chatty typing on the computer keyboard and

Kathy balancing on the curtain rod. I oohed and awwwed in the right places until she wound down. Then I gave her my spiel.

"You know it was me who interrupted the scene in the alley where Donald Hardwicke was found? Well, I just want to give my condolences to his family and see if I can answer any questions that might help them find some closure." I cringed as I said the lie. Though if they could tell me anything that would help me find the real killer, then I *would* be bringing closure, wouldn't I?

Hattie's lips tightened into a thin line. *Well, a thinner line.* Then she exhaled loudly. "Perhaps I could call up to the room."

A few minutes later, a fifty-something man stepped into the lounge where I was waiting.

"Miss Parrett?"

"Yes," I held out my hand, "thank you for seeing me, and I'm so terribly sorry about your son-in-law."

"Actually, I really don't know why you're here."

I took a deep breath. "I was there when Rooster – that's Mr. Roosevelt – was arrested. Since then, I've come to know him and I don't believe he murdered Donald. I was hoping to talk to you and your daughter and perhaps find some clue to the real killer."

Uh oh. He was looking apoplectic.

"You have some nerve. The police seem pretty certain they have the killer, but you want to drag Mary and me through the muck to save him!"

This wasn't going at all well. I soldiered on, though.

"Don't you want to be sure the real murderer is brought to justice?"

Before he could answer, another voice was heard. "I do." The speaker had a look of someone whose joy had been ripped from her, yet she held herself erect and was holding on to sanity – just. "I'm Mary Hardwicke, this is my father, Ray Gethings." She patted his arm and directed her attention at him. "It's alright, Pop. It will help if I talk about it." Turning back to me, with a lopsided smile that didn't meet her eyes she said, "Shall we sit?"

We settled ourselves around a small coffee table and I found myself telling her how I came to be in the alley, what had happened and then describing Rooster and his life.

"So you see, he's just not the kind of man who would take another life."

"You're not convincing me," Ray said. "A Vietnam vet with PTSD who's admittedly been violent in the past. Sounds like exactly the right person is behind bars."

"Pop," Mary cautioned, "he sounds like the kind of person Donny would want to help.

"Polly, thank you for telling us all this. Ask me anything you want. I'll help in any way to see justice done."

For fifteen minutes I asked every question I could think of and was disheartened with the answers. Neither Mary nor her father knew of any connection between Don and anyone in Mallowapple. They'd never heard of Mallowapple before this and Mary was sure her husband had not planned on staying here. And, no, they could think of no-one who might wish Don harm.

"He is….was…a wonderful husband and father. We have two beautiful little girls, ordinary jobs, belong to the PTA. Donny is a Rotary Club member and we like to barbeque hot dogs and hamburgers."

I was getting desperate for something of use. "Is there anything unusual that happened to him? Ever?"

Mary put her head back on the seat and raised her eyes to the ceiling. A long moment later she looked at me. "There was an incident when he was in his teens, though I don't see how it could possibly relate to this."

I widened my eyes expectantly.

"Donny and two of his friends were hunting. There was an accident and one of the kids got shot and died. Only it wasn't an accident."

"Wha… what!" Ray stiffened.

Mary gave him a guilty look. "I'm sorry, Pop. I promised I would never tell anyone, but I guess that doesn't matter anymore. Please, keep quiet 'til I get it all out."

"Go on, Mary," I said.

"They were on private land, owned by the family of the boy who was killed. They were after wild turkey but they saw a deer. The other two boys – not Donny – fired and it went down. They started arguing over who had bagged it, when suddenly, the one boy simply raised his rifle at the other and pulled the trigger.

"Donny said he was completely stunned. He was going to run for help when the other kid threatened to kill him as well unless he swore to everyone that it had been an accident. When Donny began to object, the kid said he'd just have to kill Donny's family.

"There was a big fuss, of course, and plenty of suspicion, but Donny was too terrified to tell the truth. He was only fifteen, you know. Then, a year or so later, the bad kid's family moved away."

"Do you know where?"

Mary shook her head.

"Did you know this boy?"

"No. My home was in New Hampshire. I met Donny at a sales conference in Boston and didn't move to upstate New York 'til after we married."

It was a terrible tale, but I wasn't at all sure it helped.

Ray stood, signaling an end to the conversation. Thanking them both and promising to keep in touch with any news we turned to part.

"Oh, one more thing," I said. "What was the boy's name? The one who shot his friend, that is?"

"It was John Sulkey."

I shook my head. It didn't mean a thing.

Liz Dodwell

Fifteen

In the middle of the night I awoke and sat bolt upright. I'd been dreaming that a multi-tentacled creature had been chasing me, only it had Tyler's head and was wearing a cornflower blue paisley tie. I didn't know whether to run away or stop and say, 'Take me, I'm yours.' Apparently the sleeping me decided it was best to give up on the whole sequence and so here I was, wide awake and fidgety.

Sighing, I extricated myself from the bed between a host of furry bodies. Vinny half-opened one eye and Taz complained because I had to move her a teensy weensy bit. Other than that, the whole gang slept on.

My mind wouldn't settle down, so I decided I may as well put it to good use. Opening up the laptop I tried to organize my thoughts in print. All I did was end up with a page of rambling ideas and very few hard facts. Looking over the notes the name John Sulkey jumped out at me. Curious to know more about the incident I ran a search, adding in Hardwicke's name, home town and the year the killing happened.

A few articles popped up about a teen accidentally shooting his friend. They didn't tell me more than I already knew and there were no pictures of the kids, presumably because they were underage. For the heck of it I ran a general search for John Sulkey with the town name, and bingo! Up popped a picture of the junior varsity high school football team. Sulkey was listed as the seventh from the left in the back row. I zoomed in on the face. The quality was really grainy and it was a small image to begin with, but as I peered closely I understood what it means to say your blood runs cold.

It took me a few moments to get over the shock. Then, without thinking, I snatched up the phone and hit speed-dial for Tyler.

"Polly?" The voice was groggy. Hell, I hadn't realized it was three thirty in the morning. *Oops.* Then the tone became alarmed. "Polly. Are you OK? I can be right over if you need me." *Well, that was gratifying. He really must care.*

"Polly! Say something!"

"I'm OK, everything's fine. It's more than fine. I think I know what happened to Don Hardwicke."

Sixteen

The coffee maker coughed out the last of the fresh pot. Coffee was one of the few things I always had on hand. Fortunately, everyone took it black, as there was no milk or sugar to go with it.

It was mid-morning. Tyler, Zill Granger and Sheriff Wisniewski sat around the kitchen table. We'd been talking for over an hour. Wisniewski had objected to meeting at my place but Granger had managed to persuade him it was for the best. Now he sat taut, palpable waves of anger coursing from his body.

Tyler had arrived on my doorstep soon after I'd called him. When I opened the door he'd crushed me in a warm embrace. "Don't ever scare me like that again."

I acted innocent. "What do you mean?"

"You can't call me in the early hours of the morning without scaring me. There's a killer out there. I thought you were in danger." *Wow. This was more than gratifying.*

"Sorry," I mumbled.

I'd gone through my notes and my theory with Tyler, who then called the attorney. Granger came right over and I went through everything again. Then Granger contacted the sheriff and I'd repeated my hypothesis for the third time. Wisniewski had confirmed one thing we weren't sure of – the time of death. As far as I was concerned, that pretty much sealed the deal.

"There's still no hard evidence," Wisniewski said.

"But now you have enough to check DNA and fingerprints against another suspect." Granger gave the sheriff a hard look.

"I'm going to take care of that as soon as I get to my office. Fingerprint samples will be on file, but it will take a while for the DNA."

"Is this enough to get Rooster out on bail?" Tyler asked.

"That's for a judge to decide," Granger responded, "but I think there's a good chance."

"What more do we need?" I was probably on my eighth cup of coffee, so I was a little excitable.

"Let me check it off for you again:

a. We now know Hardwicke's body was most likely in the dumpster at nine, when Tyler and I came upon Rooney playing Robocop with Rooster and Elaine.

b. Hardwicke left Bennie's Diner suddenly, right after he saw Rooney. That suggests he followed Rooney out.

c. Elaine growled at Rooney – twice. In fact, she growled both times she saw him and she never growls at anyone. *That* suggests she senses something bad about him.

d. Officer Anson Rooney is John Sulkey. That's his face in the high school picture. So, not only is he a known killer, the photo puts him in the same school, at the same time, as Don Hardwicke."

"Young lady, a dog growling will not get a conviction. I am going to pull Rooney in for questioning and put him on suspension. If there's a fingerprint match then that's a whole different ballgame." Wisniewski stood. "Thank you for the coffee. Now I'm going to get on with my job."

It wasn't much longer before Granger left. Tyler headed out soon after with a promise to call later. We all had work to get on with. Fortunately, my injured sitter was back on the job and I'd been able to re-arrange my schedule to clear the morning.

As I was setting off on my rounds a call came in from Suzette. "Polly, can I ask a big favor?"

She'd taken Elaine to the vet for a check-up and come outside to find her car wouldn't start.

"I'm waiting for a tow-truck now, but could you come and get Elaine? I don't want to drag her to the repair shop or leave her at the vet's. She'll be happier with you."

"No problem. I'm only a few minutes away. I'll head over now."

I settled Elaine in the front seat as Suzette's car was hooked up. We exchanged a quick hug and she promised that she or Tyler would swing by in the evening.

I enjoyed having my sweet friend with me again and she seemed to enjoy riding around. We only had a couple more stops to make when a call came in. I didn't recognize the number but, when you're in my business, you always answer.

Liz Dodwell

"Pets and People, Too. This is Polly, can I help a pet or a person today?"

"This is Sheriff Wisniewski. Polly, it looks like you're right about Rooney. We matched his fingerprints."

I slapped the dashboard in glee and yelped.

"It's not all good." *Uh, oh.* "Rooney must have got wind something was going on and he's disappeared."

"Disappeared? You mean as in he's run away?"

"I mean we haven't been able to find him. He ditched his squad car, he's not responding to calls and he's not at his apartment. There's a BOLO out on him but I need you to be careful."

"What do you mean by careful?" I squeaked. "Am I in danger?"

Wisniewski tried to reassure me. "I'm only saying you should take sensible precautions. Keep your eyes peeled and keep your doors locked."

That didn't sound very reassuring.

"Have you told Tyler?"

"I left a message for him. Apparently, he's with clients."

"OK, sheriff. Thanks, I guess."

"If you see or hear anything, you call right away."

With that he hung up and I was left feeling nervous and unsure. There wasn't much I could do, though, except finish my visits and get home.

It was a relief when I pulled into my driveway, though not when I saw my automatic light wasn't on. Six o'clock hadn't come yet, but the sun had set long before and it was really dark. I felt horribly vulnerable. *Why didn't I carry a gun?* Of course, I had no idea how to use one. Perhaps I should rectify that.

Telling myself to stop being such a wuss, I got out of the van and went round to open the door for Elaine. With key in hand we approached the door when Elaine stopped in her tracks. She stiffened and started to growl. *Oh, hell.* I knew what that meant. Rooney was here.

I hesitated, not knowing whether to run back to the van or rush for the door. But Elaine didn't hesitate at all. She charged forward as Rooney stepped from the bushes, raising his pistol at her. The only things I had were the keys and the dog leash. I flung the keys at Rooney's head and caught him right in the eye. Instinctively, he reached upward and the gun discharged harmlessly in the air.

Now Elaine had him by the leg. He turned the gun back to her and I cracked the leash at his hand like a whip. Unbelievably, it jerked the gun from his grip. I was beginning to feel like a regular Indiana Jones.

With his free leg, Rooney kicked savagely at Elaine's head. Without so much as a whimper she went down. Enraged, I hurled myself at him and we both fell to the ground. I clawed and bit but he was bigger and a lot stronger than me, and maybe just as desperate. My arms were pinned behind me and a knee to my stomach knocked the wind out of me – hard. I gagged and struggled for breath as he flipped me over so I was eating dirt. With his weight on me, I couldn't move or breathe. Then I felt something round my neck. Even as I was already losing consciousness, I realized it was the leash.

Thoughts of my mother, my dogs, my cats and Elaine flashed through my brain and I tried even harder to fight but my efforts became weaker and weaker. Suddenly I was bathed in a white light. *So this is it. This is what dying is like.*

Seventeen

Eww. Tyler needed breath mints if he was going to keep kissing me. I reached out to push his face away. *When did he start growing facial hair?*

I opened my eyes. Angel was looking right at me and my head hurt like hell. Come to think of it, my whole body hurt. "She's awake," I heard someone say.

"Thank God." That was Tyler's voice. He moved into my vision. "You're safe now. We got him. You'll be OK."

I wondered what he was talking about, then it came to me in a rush. I couldn't help myself; I burst into tears and clung to him tighter than a limpet to a rock. Then I thought of Elaine.

"She's awake but she's been taken to the emergency vet, just in case."

I heard another voice announce the arrival of the ambulance. "Who's hurt?" I asked.

"You. You're going to the hospital to get checked out. That was quite a beating Rooney gave you."

"I don't understand what happened."

"I know. I'll explain everything later. Right now I'm going to let the EMTs take care of you.

That was pretty much it for me until I woke in a hospital bed with my mother beside me, holding my hand.

"Polly Parrett, you do make life difficult for me," but she smiled as she said it and I smiled back. Or tried to; my jaw didn't want to cooperate.

"You're lucky. It's not broken, but the bone is badly bruised. The doctor says there will be a lot of swelling and a good bit of pain for quite some time."

"It doesn't feel painful now."

"That's the drugs," Mom said. "You also have a couple of broken ribs and a lot of scrapes and bruises and can expect a very sore throat. And there's a terrible bruise around your neck where....." Mom's eyes glossed with tears and her breathing started to get ragged.

"Where Rooney tried to strangle me," I said softly.

Mom nodded and bit her lip. I waited for her to compose herself. Considering the circumstances, I was surprised I was so mellow. Must be another effect of the drugs.

I wanted to know about Elaine, and who was taking care of my own creatures.

"As far as I know, Elaine is fine. I called one of your sitters and they have everything else in hand. They'll take it in turns to stay at your house as long as need be and they'll cover all your own visits, so you're not to worry." *I have a wonderful crew.* "I also called your father and he'll be here today."

"You actually talked to dad?"

"Whatever else I may think, he's still your father and deserves to know what's happened. He said he'll stay as long as you need him and do whatever he can to help. Now, I'm supposed to call the nurse when you wake." She pushed her chair away from the bed.

"Wait a minute. You have to tell me what happened."

"Tyler happened. And that's all I can say right now without falling apart."

I drifted in and out of sleep. At one point when I awoke, Wisniewski was there with a female officer to question me. He was surprisingly considerate and when he was finished I said, "I need you tell me what happened last night." And so he did.

Rooney had deliberately broken the driveway light and hidden at the side of the house, waiting for me to get home. Of course, he'd had no idea that Elaine was with me. The sheriff believed his plan was simply to shoot me. *Rooney seemed to like that modus operandi.*

The white light I'd thought was my pathway to another life, was actually the headlights of Tyler's car. He hadn't got the sheriff's message alerting him to Rooney's escape. Meanwhile, Suzette had asked him to collect Elaine. He'd arrived in time to pull Rooney off me and save the day. When the police arrived, they found Tyler cradling me in his arms, with Rooney out cold.

"If you think you look bad," *I didn't think that. How bad did I look?* "you should see Rooney. Tyler really did a number on him. He must have been one angry man." *That was so sweet.*

Apparently, after Tyler had given me up safely to the EMTs, he'd driven out to collect my mother and bring her to the hospital and had stayed with her, and me, through most of the night. He left in the morning when he had to retrieve Elaine from the emergency vet.

"So she's alright?"

"She had a relatively mild concussion. Nothing that should cause any permanent damage."

This day was getting better and better, but I still didn't know *why* Rooney had killed his old friend. The sheriff explained.

"Once we got Rooney in custody, he let it all out. He seems to think he's justified in everything he did."

"He's wacko."

"I won't argue with that. Anyway, Hardwicke recognized Rooney in the diner. He followed Rooney out and accosted him, saying he'd been quiet long enough and it was time for the truth to be told. Rooney persuaded him to step into the alley where they could talk. You'd think Hardwicke would have known better, but he practically signed his own death warrant right then.

"Rooney had to do something quickly but knew he'd attract attention if he fired his gun. So he picked up a brick and smashed Hardwicke's head, then heaved him into the dumpster, hoping the body wouldn't be found for at least a few days.

"That's when Rooster came along. He had no idea what had happened – though apparently Elaine knew something. Anyway, the last thing Rooney needed was someone opening the dumpster where he'd just hidden the body."

"So he had to come up with an excuse to get Rooster out of the way," I injected.

"Exactly. Luckily for Rooster, you and Breslin showed up."

It was a case of being in the right place at the right time.

Liz Dodwell

Eighteen

I was in hospital for a total of three days. Dad had arrived and spent his time between the hospital room and my place, taking over pet-care duties there. I was really happy to see my parents getting along. Perhaps Mom had finally put her angst behind her.

There was a steady stream of visitors. Both my brothers turned up, my crew members stopped in to reassure me that all was well, Suzette popped in a couple of times and Tyler came to see me. I found myself feeling awkward and shy around him; I didn't know what to say. Happily, Mom filled the gap and showered him with gratitude to the point that *he* appeared awkward and shy.

When I was discharged it was with a lot of painkillers and instructions to take it easy. Not too bad for someone who was nearly killed.

It was decided – not by me – that I would stay with Mom until I was completely healed. That was sort of like the blind leading the blind under the circumstances, but I acquiesced and my four-pawed gang and I made the move. Dad stayed for a few more days, using my house as his base, and ran errands and fussed over both of us. It was nice.

The best thing that happened was Rooster's release. While I was still hospitalized he was freed and joined his beloved Elaine at Tyler's home. I wished I'd been there to see the reunion. On the second day at Mom's Tyler brought them out for a visit. It was very emotional. We all shed a few tears, Rooster most of all, thanking us for caring for a 'worthless stranger' and his old dog.

When things calmed down, Mom and I headed to the kitchen to make tea. Dad had the presence of mind to buy a good bottle of sherry, so we added that to the mix.

"You know what struck me?" Mom said. "Rooster referring to himself as worthless. It's so sad he should feel that way. He's obviously a good person."

"Perhaps we can find a way to help," I said. "I remember Tyler told me the VA had offered to do what they could and I'm sure that hasn't changed. Rooster is a proud man, though. He won't accept anything if he thinks it's charity."

I set a plate of gingerbread cookies and brandy-soaked Christmas cake on Mom's lap and followed her with the tea and sherry as she wheeled her way back to the living room. We were all chatting when the heat came on with its usual squealing and sputtering. Mom gave her usual apology, "It's been that way for years."

"I can probably fix it for you," Rooster said.

Dad immediately told him not to worry about it, but Mom and I looked at each other, then Mom turned to Rooster and asked, "How are you at house painting?"

Nineteen

Christmas Day

It had snowed heavily overnight. I looked through the window and it seemed as if our house had been wrapped in silvery white paper, like a present under the tree. Inside was the gift of warm Christmas colors, a cheerful fire, the scent of cinnamon, nutmeg, and pine from the freshly cut garlands; all mixed with a generous amount of laughter and love.

My brothers had arrived a couple of days earlier. Keene's wife, Megan was with him of course, and Seb had brought a girlfriend. There was no doubt the relationship was serious and I took to Ellie right away.

The guys strung the house with lights of red, blue and green. They'd found the perfect tree, which had been decked with the old ornaments I'd found in the attic. To be clear, I should say the *upper* part of the tree had been decorated. Bright, shiny objects are wonderful, but potentially dangerous toys to kitties and pooches. It looked a bit odd, I suppose, but to us it was still beautiful.

Rooster was with us too, and Elaine, of course. Since Rooster had fixed the heating, he'd started painting and doing other odd jobs for Mom. Rather than drive him back and forth from Tyler's, Mom had suggested he stay in one of the spare rooms. It was working out great. Not only was stuff getting taken care of, it was a real boost to Rooster's sense of self-worth and Mom was enjoying the company.

We'd put presents under the tree for Rooster and his faithful companion. Not surprisingly, Rooster got teary-eyed when he pulled out the aran sweater we'd got for him and read the card packaged with it: 'Friends are the family you choose. Welcome to our family.'

Elaine didn't know what to make of her gift. My dogs have as much fun ripping the paper off the packages as they do with their new toys. So Rooster pulled the paper apart to reveal a big beef-flavored chewie, which Elaine took very gently while her tail waved energetically.

What a perfect Christmas this was. Well, almost. As I looked around the room at Keene and Megan, Seb and Ellie, Mom and Rooster, a wave of loneliness swept over me. Try as I might to put Tyler from my mind, I couldn't help but wish there was something more to our relationship. He'd been invited to join us but declined, saying his family always spent Christmas at their timeshare in Bermuda.

"Polly," Mom called. "Give me a hand in the kitchen while the others set the table."

Dutifully, I headed for the kitchen. Megan and Ellie joined us and we pulled the turkey from the oven, popped the sweet potato casserole under the grill to brown the marshmallows, stirred the homemade cranberry sauce and drizzled a little more olive oil over the roast asparagus. When everything was ready we carried it into the dining room. By the time we were finished the table looked magnificent and the smells had me drooling almost as much as the dogs.

"There's one too many settings," I pointed out.

"I don't think so," Mom said.

"There are seven of us and we have eight settings. I'll clear it."

"No, dear. We're going to need it."

At that very moment the dogs jumped up in unison and dashed to the door as the bell chimed.

"Why don't you get that, Polly?"

Everyone was looking at me as if they knew something I didn't. *I hate that.* Hesitantly, I went to the door.

"Enough!" I said to silence the dogs. "Back!" I pointed to their blanket and obediently they moved back and stood there. "Stay!"

I opened the door and the dogs launched themselves at the man standing there. He might have been able to keep his footing if the porch had been shoveled and salted, but it hadn't. Instead it was slick as an ice-rink. The man's legs went out from under him and down he went, the bag he'd had in hand emptying its contents of prettily packed boxes into the snow.

"Tyler!"

The dogs were happily dishing big wet kisses on his face and plopping wet paws over his Arcteryx jacket.

"Off," I shrieked, "Off," trying to pull Angel away and lift Coco into my arms. Instead, my feet went in all directions and I fell onto my back next to Tyler. Mortified, I turned my face to his. For several seconds we looked at each other, then he burst into laughter. Before I knew it, I was laughing with him.

Together we hauled ourselves up and gathered the gifts.

Liz Dodwell

"What are you doing here? You're supposed to be in Bermuda."

"There was something I really wanted to bring you."

From his pocket he drew a slightly crushed sprig of mistletoe. Holding it up high he pulled me to him with his free arm and kissed me. A real kiss. *Merry Christmas to me.*

You're probably thinking that's the end. Well, it's not. After we'd settled ourselves around the table Mom chinked her glass and announced, "Before we eat, I have something to say.

"More than bringing the Christmas holiday back to this house, you've brought the spirit. I've been reminded of how it feels to be part of a family and of the things you can accomplish together.

"For the past couple of years I've been absorbed in a misery of my own making. That's going to change. I want to get back to work and I want to do something that will benefit others.

"Rooster and I have been talking." We all glanced at him, wondering what was going on.

"He tells me there are lots of homeless vets, with pets, who just want a chance to get back to a normal life. I want to give them that chance. I want to make this home a sort of half-way house for those people. I know it's a huge undertaking, but Rooster has agreed to stay, and between us all I believe we can make this work."

There was a stunned silence.

Seb, Keene and I began to object but Mom raised her hand. "I don't want to hear anything negative. All of you, please, think on it and we can discuss it after the holidays. For now, let's just make this the merriest of Christmases."

"I'll second that," Tyler said, raising his glass. "And I would be proud to help in any way." *He is the greatest guy.*

We all raised our glasses with him and chinked them together. "Merry Christmas," everyone said, and lying in front of the fire Elaine gave us a doggy grin and thumped her tail loudly on the floor.

Get a FREE book!

This is the first in the Polly Parrett series. If you'd like to be among the first to know of new releases and special deals and get a FREE short story that's not published anywhere, just go here:

http://lizdodwell.com/freestory/

Get the next books in the Polly Parrett Pet-Sitter Cozy Mystery series.

The Christmas Kitten
Bird Brain
Erik the Red (due April 2016)

Other books by Liz Dodwell:

Chaplain Merriman cozy series:
Christmas Can Be Murder
Deadly Confession

Captain Finn Treasure Mysteries:
The Mystery of the One-Armed Man (Book 1)
Black Bart is Dead (Book 2)
The Gold Doubloon Mystery (Book 3)
The Game's a Foot (Book 4)
Captain Finn Boxed Set (Books 1-3)

Author's Notes

Hi, dear readers. I hope you enjoyed reading about Polly and her family – including the furry kind – as much as I enjoyed writing about them. If so, please consider leaving a review wherever you purchased this book. As an independent author it's not easy to compete out there, and your feedback will help me know what you like. I'd also love to get to know you on my facebook page:

http://www.facebook.com/LizDodwellAuthor

Join me there and tell me about your own pets or funny pet-sitting stories. I check there every day and answer all questions – honest!

Now, to thank some people. First of all, you, my readers, without whom there would be no Polly Parrett. I can't tell you how much I appreciate your support.

Much gratitude also to Dominic Ottaviano, my multi-tasking assistant; to Tracy Nowell, a truly lovely lady and invaluable helper; and my husband, Alex Markovich, as always, for constant support and faith in my abilities.

Liz Dodwell devotes her time to writing and publishing from the home she shares with husband, Alex and a host of rescued dogs and cats, collectively known as "the kids." She will tell you, "I gladly suffer the luxury of working from home where I'm with my "kids," can toss in a load of laundry in between radio interviews, writing, editing, general office work or baking pupcakes (dog treats) while still in my PJs. I love what I do and know how lucky I am to be able to do it. Oh, and if you asked me what my hobbies are, I'd probably say reading murder mysteries, drinking champagne, romantic dinners with my husband and yodeling (just joking about that last one)."

CPSIA information can be obtained
at www.ICGtesting.com
Printed in the USA
LVOW04s1915261016

510378LV00015B/107/P

9 781939 860163